Geronimo Stilton

HEROMICE

DINOSAUR DANGER

Scholastic Inc.

Published by Scholastic Inc., 557 Broadway, New York, NY 10012.

SCHOLASTIC and associated logos are trademarks and/or registered trademarks of Scholastic Inc.

ISBN 978-1-338-05288-6

Text by Geronimo Stilton
Original title *Polpette di supertopo per il T-Rex*
Original design of the Heromice world by Giuseppe Facciotto and Flavio Ferron
Cover by Giuseppe Facciotto (design) and Daniele Verzini (color)
Illustrations by Luca Usai (pencils), Valeria Cairoli (inks), and Daniele Verzini (color)
Graphics by Chiara Cebraro and Francesca Sirianni

Special thanks to Joanne Ruelos Diaz
Translated by Andrea Schaffer
Interior design by Kevin Callahan / BNGO Books

First printing, September 2016 by Scholastic Malaysia, operating under Grolier (Malaysia) Sdn. Bhd.,
Printed in Malaysia

When darkness falls over Muskrat City, the Sewer Rats slither into the alleys to cause chaos aboveground. But the citizens of Muskrat City know that there are mysterious figures watching over them, ready to fight evil at all costs.
They are strong, they are invincible, they are fearless — well, almost . . .
They are the Heromice!

Nothing is impossible for the Heromice!

MEET THE HEROMICE!

GERONIMO SUPERSTILTON

The strongest hero in Muskrat City . . . but he still must learn how to control his powers!

SWIFTPAWS

Geronimo Superstilton's partner in crimefighting; he can transform his supersuit into anything.

LADY WONDERWHISKERS

A mysterious mouse with special powers; she always seems to be in the right place at the right time.

TESS TECHNOPAWS

A cook and scientist who assists the Heromice with every mission.

ELECTRON AND PROTON

Supersmart mouselets who help the Heromice; they create and operate sophisticated technological gadgets.

TONY SLUDGE

The undisputed leader of the Sewer Rats; known for being tough and mean.

SLICKFUR

Sludge's right-hand mouse; the true (and only) brains behind the Sewer Rats.

TERESA SLUDGE

Tony's wife; makes the important decisions for their family.

ONE, TWO, AND THREE

Bodyguards who act as Sludge's henchmice; they are big, buff, and brainless.

ELENA SLUDGE

Tony and Teresa's teenage daughter; has a real weakness for rat metal music.

A Day at the Mouseum

It was a **picture-perfect** day in New Mouse City and I was on my way to the Mouseum of Modern Art. I couldn't wait to see the latest exhibit by the hottest artist of the century, Andy Mousehol! His work is **pawsitively** genius!

Oh, excuse me! I haven't even introduced myself. My name is *Geronimo Stilton*, and I am the editor of *The Rodent's Gazette*, the most **FAMOUSE** newspaper on Mouse Island!

As I was saying, I was on my way to the exhibit's opening gala. I had to write a front-page article about Mousehol for the *Gazette*.

When I arrived at the mouseum, Andy

Mousehol was in the garden, surrounded by ADMIRERS. They were marveling at his latest creation, *Gorgonzola Gorge Part 5*. It looked like . . . a **pile of washing machines**!

I was just imagining how my article would look next to a photograph of this **must-see** masterpiece when

rrrriiiinnnggg!

My cell phone rang.

"Hello? Superstilton, are you there?!"

Hmm . . .

It sounded like my friend Hercule Poirat, also known as Swiftpaws. You see, sometimes (even though I don't

want to be!), I'm a Heromouse. Swiftpaws is my superpartner. "Swiftpaws, is that you?"

"**GREAT GLOBS OF GOAT CHEESE!**" he bellowed. "You must get to the Mouseum of Natural History in Muskrat City right away!"

"N-n-natural H-h-history?" I squeaked. "You must be mistaken. I'm at the Mouseum of Modern—"

"There's no mistaking it!" he said. "We need you right away! There's an emergency of **prehistoric** proportions!"

"P-p-prehistoric?" My tail immediately began to tremble. I'm really not cut out to be a Heromouse! "But I'm a little busy —"

Swiftpaws paid me no attention.

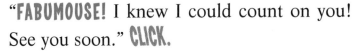
"FABUMOUSE! I knew I could count on you! See you soon." CLICK.

I sighed. There was only one thing I could do. Swiftpaws needed me, or rather, he needed Superstilton. I looked around for a place to change into my supersuit and saw an old phone booth on the far side of the garden. I DARTED over and was just about to push the SECRET button on the Superpen when I heard a voice.

"And WHAT are YOU doing in here?" someone boomed.

I zipped around. GULP! It was the famouse Andy Mousehol right there in the fur!

"Who, me? I . . . was just . . . making a telephone call . . ." I stammered.

"A telephone call?" Mousehol said incredulously. "This is my most famouse

5

piece, **Dial M for Muenster**. You don't know it?!"

GREAT BALLS OF MOZZARELLA!

I had mistaken his masterpiece for an actual **telephone booth**! As humiliated as I was, there was no time to lose. I scurried away and pressed the **secret** button on

Get out of my masterpiece!

Pardon me!

the Superpen. A GREEN light scanned me from tail to whiskers, transforming me into Superstilton!

Powered by my *supersuit*, I flew off and landed moments later in front of Muskrat City's Mouseum of Natural History. My paws had barely touched the ground when Swiftpaws called out, "You took long enough, superpartner!"

On my way!

"What's the emergency?" I asked in a panic. "Is **fondue** flooding the streets? Has the cheddar gone missing from the all-you-can-eat cheese buffet?!"

"Worse, Superstilton! We're late!"

"L-late? Late for what?"

"For the opening gala of the latest exhibit,

7

of course. They can't start without us—we're the ***guests of honor***!"

Wait a second. I had just 𝖆𝖇𝖆𝖓𝖉𝖔𝖓𝖊𝖉 a mouseum gala! And was there 𝖋𝖚𝖗 in my ears or had I heard correctly? How could I be a **guest of honor** at an event I hadn't known about?

A Prehistoric Surprise

As we entered the mouseum, Swiftpaws explained himself.

"**Wow!** Mayor Pete Powerpaws invited us?" I exclaimed.

"Of course!" said Swiftpaws. "You're a Heromouse. You're a big cheese in Muskrat City!"

The thought made my whiskers twitch. After all, *I'm not cut out to be a Heromouse!* But before I could say another word, I tripped and found my snout inches away from the largest claws I had ever seen! When I looked up, I saw they were part of a **GIGANTIC DINOSAUR!**

"It looks *real*, doesn't it?" Swiftpaws murmured.

So real, my heart had practically leaped out of my fur! "These models are the most realistic ones I've ever seen!" I exclaimed.

"I'll take that as a compliment!" said a voice behind us.

We turned to see a rodent wearing a vest full of POCKETS, a leather bag, and an explorer's hat.

"I'm Professor Tyler Ratosaurus and the curator of this exhibit," he continued, shaking my paw. "You must be Superstilton."

"Yes, nice to meet you!"

"Professor Ratosaurus is a famous PALEONTOLOGY scholar and the leading expert on dinosaurs," added a feminine voice.

I turned and gasped.

"Lady Wonderwhiskers!" Swiftpaws squeaked. "You're here, too?!"

"How could I miss it?" the **captivating** super-rodent replied.

The professor strode over and kissed her paw. He seemed *DAZZLED* by the Heromouse's intelligence, confidence, and STUNNING blue eyes (well, who isn't?).

Welcome!

Hello!

"It's a real pleasure to meet you, Lady Wonderwhiskers," the professor said. "May I accompany you to your seat?" And with that, he WHISKED her away.

In the meantime, the room was filling with visitors.

"Hi, Superstilton!" chirped two voices in the crowd.

It was Proton and ELECTRON, young mouselets and valued friends to the Heromice. "We're here with our school," Electron explained.

Proton looked at me expectantly. "Are you ReaDY?"

Something was starting to STINK. "R-ready? F-for what?"

"Ah! Well . . ." Swiftpaws responded. "There is a tiny thing I, ahem, forgot to tell you . . ."

I sighed. What mess had Swiftpaws gotten me into this time?

"Have no fear, Superstilton," Swiftpaws was saying as something caught my eye. I recognized those ears. That snout looked familiar. Was I looking in the **MIRROR**? No, it was a flyer — featuring my face!

SUPERSTILTON
Honored guest
and
Mousespeaker

I wasn't prepared for this!

"It's no **BIG** deal, Superstilton. The mayor asked that you give a forty-five-minute **speech** to the mouseum's two hundred guests," my superpartner chattered.

"WHAAAAAT?!"

A forty-five-minute speech!

Mayor Powerpaws was already making his way to the podium on the stage. My stomach sank faster than a bowling ball in a crock of fondue.

"But I haven't prepared any SPEECH," I squeaked.

Swiftpaws laughed. "You'll be fine! Look, I prepared notes for you." With that, he pulled a RAT'S NEST of crumpled papers from his pocket.

A Live Exhibit

I **ruffled** through the notes as Swiftpaws ushered me to the stage. But I couldn't read a word! It was as if a mouseling had written them in **string cheese**! As I stood in front of the **enormouse** crowd, the notes **slipped** from my paws.

What a **DISASTER**! I cleared my throat and squeaked, "Uh . . . W-w-welcome . . . to . . . uh . . ."

As sweat dripped from my snout, Proton watched from the center of the room.

Thump!

I saw someone shove a baby stroller into Proton's side.

"Pay attention, **pipsqueak**!" grumbled a massive rodent.

"Oh! I'm sorry—I didn't see you!" Proton said in confusion.

"You could have woken our princess," whined the rodent's wife.

Electron went over to see what had happened.

"Is everything okay?" she asked.

But the mother rat **ignored** her.

"Let's go, my little dearie," the mother cooed to the stroller. Then she looked back and called behind her. "You, too, Elen — I mean, uh . . . **Fiona!**"

Proton glanced over as a young rodent strolled by, rolling her eyes. "Yes, Mom . . ."

"Hmm . . ." commented Electron. "I know that **voice** . . ." With a quick look to Proton, the two followed the *family* across the room.

A moment later, the **stocky** rodent

STOPPED and leaned over the stroller. Proton and Electron hid behind a dinosaur statue and watched as he lifted out a MYSTERIOUS multicolored device instead of a cute little baby!

"Everybody, FREEZE!" roared the

rat. Then he aimed the device at the crowd.

Electron's fur stood on end. "Stop where you are!" she shouted as she leaped from her hiding spot. "I know you!

Huh?!

Everybody, freeze!

You're the Sludge family!"

Melted Muenster on a muffin!

"The Sludge family?!" exclaimed the mayor.

At that, the father rodent swiped off his SUNGLASSES. It was Tony Sludge, the head of Muskrat City's evil Sewer Rats!

"You guessed it, **runt**," he growled at Electron.

"What are you doing here, Sludge?!" cried Commissioner Rex Ratford.

"Oh, nothing much . . ." He smirked. "I just wanted to see the DINOSAURS."

Then he pointed the device at the model of a velociraptor.

I watched from the stage in horror as a **blue** light shot out of the contraption and hit the center of the dinosaur.

SUPER SWISS SCRAMBLED EGGS!

The humongous reptile roared to life, rattling the mouseum windows. The beast then **leaped** off the pedestal with its **JAWS** wide-open, sending mouseum visitors scurrying in all directions.

"Oh no!" Electron gasped.

Proton nodded, his whiskers **SHAKING**. "This is a **gigantosaurus** disaster," he whispered to his friend.

Meanwhile, I was frozen in fear on the stage. But I was jolted out of my stupor when someone called my *name*.

"Do something, Superstilton!" yelled a mouse in the crowd.

"The Heromice will **SAVE** us!" shouted another.

Tony started laughing. "Heh, heh, heh! I **doubt** it," he scoffed. "Please allow me to present the Animatronic Laser Ray! This **little gadget** transforms these worthless inanimate models into *dangerous predators*!" He scanned our terrified faces and sneered. "And guess what, rodents? The **best** is yet to come!"

THE GREAT ESCAPE

Tony launched another **flurry** of **blue** lights into the atrium. Blasted by the Animatronic Laser Ray, the models sprang to life.

The **velociraptors** thundered down the stairs. The **brontosauruses** swung their tails, shaking the walls. The pterodactyls soared down the corridors, spreading panic through the crowd.

"Everyone get to the emergency exits!" shouted Mayor Powerpaws.

I alone remained on the stage, **immobilized** by fear! For the love of cheese rinds! **NOW WHAT?**

"Prehistoric provolone poppers!" shouted Swiftpaws, calling after the evil rodents.

"**STOP** where you are, Sludges!"

Tony laughed maniacally. "Nice try, Heromice! You can't stop my SUPERDINOSAURS!"

"You and your reptiles will

see what the **Heromice** can do!" Lady Wonderwhiskers retorted.

I hoped she meant **HIDE** under a chair and whimper. I know I'm supposed to be a hero, but I'm still a **MOUSE**! And I'd never seen anything as **scary** as

those rodent-loving, prehistoric beasts! But before I could find a hiding spot, we heard a booming rooooaaarrr!

The snarl of a velociraptor made Tony jump. The dino was approaching him; his wife, Teresa; and their daughter, Elena; SNIFFING hungrily.

"Daddy, are you sure the SUPERDINOSAURS are under our control?" asked Elena.

"Of course I'm sure, darling," Tony replied confidently. "Don't you trust your dear old dad?"

"Sludgy, I'm not sure these reptiles like us very much. I think we'd better get out of here . . ." Teresa said. She eyed the dinosaur suspiciously.

Then she and Elena started backing away.

Raaahhhrrrggg!

The roaring reptile stormed toward them.

"Retreeeaaat!"

yelled the Sewer Rats' leader. He dropped the laser ray and scurried at top speed toward the exit.

Swiftpaws tried to follow them, but the velociraptor's tail struck him, **KNOCKING** him into the air at **SUPERSONIC SPEED**. "Supersuit: Pillow Mode!"

With those words, he transformed into a **pillow**

Pillow mode!

just before CRASHING into a wall.

POOF!
BOIIING!

Swiftpaws **superbounced** off the wall, landing with a soft **THUMP**.

Meanwhile, the brave Lady Wonderwhiskers **whisked** the visitors out of the exits.

How brave!
Such courage!
What a mouse!

I was running toward her when I heard a mouselet's CRY.

"Superstilton, HELP!"

Electron and her classmates were trapped in a corner by a towering BRONTOSAURUS.

"I'm coming!" I yelled.

With a *superleap*, I bounded over, but the brontosaurus was just as quick. I darted to the side and barely avoided being squashed under its gigantic foot.

"Mighty Mesozoic manchego!" I shouted.

At the sound of those words, my superpowers activated. Suddenly, wheels of manchego cheese RAINED down, completely surrounding the reptile in a cheesy cage. He was TRAPPED — for the moment anyway. Electron and her friends were able to *escape* through the exit (escorted by yours truly). Whew.

Mission accomplished!

SUPERPOWER:
CAGE OF MESOZOIC MANCHEGO
ACTIVATED WITH THE CRY:
"MIGHTY MESOZOIC MANCHEGO!"

Dinosaurs in the City

If Tony's plan was to **wreak havoc** throughout the city, it was working! Within minutes, downtown was crawling with dinosaurs. Velociraptors **STOMPED** on city buses, pterodactyls **swooped** through the sky, and brontosauruses swung their massive tails, knocking over cars.

I felt like I was at the movies, watching *Jurassic Spark 2: Dinosaur Inferno* in 3-D! But this was no film — this was real life, and I was scared out of my fur.

Commissioner Ratford tried to block off the nearby streets to contain the dinosaurs.

"But how do we **capture** them?!" he said worriedly. "They need to be stopped!"

"They act just like **real** dinosaurs!" Tyler Ratosaurus exclaimed. He watched with a mixture of **fear** and **fascination** as two triceratops locked horns with each other.

"Professor, stay close!" Commissioner Ratford shouted. "We may need your **expertise** to stop them!"

Real dinosaurs!

Just then Tess Technopaws, the **COOK** and **SUPERSCIENTIST** from **Heromice Headquarters**, came running toward Electron and me.

"**SWEET FISH STEW FONDUE!**" Tess cried. "Are you okay? I scampered over as soon as I heard." She glanced around. "Where's **PROTON**?"

Electron stared at her **communicator watch** and frowned. "I lost sight of him while I was scurrying out. I called him, but he's not responding."

"Let's hope he isn't in **tROUBLe!**" Tess said worriedly.

"*Sizzling Swiss on a stick!*" Swiftpaws exclaimed as he joined the conversation. "Who might be in trouble?"

"We can't find Proton," I yelped.

"We'll fly over the area and look for him," Swiftpaws said. "Let's hurry, superpartner!

Eek. That was easier said than done! The sky was full of pterodactyls!

"B-b-but . . ." I stammered, looking up. "Those '**birds**' don't look too friendly. And I get so **airsick** . . ."

How many times did I have to tell him? *I'm not cut out to be a Heromouse!*

"Great Jurassic jellybeans, Superstilton!" Swiftpaws replied. "There's no time to waste!"

Vrooooom!

Suddenly, we heard a large **rumbling** coming from a nearby alley. Forget about pterodactyls — Swiftpaws and I soon found ourselves snout-to-engine with the SLUDGEMOBILE!

SLICKFUR, Tony's right-hand mouse, and his bodyguards, ONE, TWO, and THREE, vaulted out of the car along with Tony and Teresa.

Swiftpaws calmly stroked his tail. "Well, well. Look who's here: the Sewer Rats!" he squeaked. "Leaving in a hurry, I see. You'll have to deal with the **Heromice** first!"

"The Heromice in full force!" exclaimed

Lady Wonderwhiskers as she joined us.

What a mouse! The super-rodent of my **dreams** always seems to be right there when I need her.

The Sludgemobile!

Ready, superpartner?

"Ha!" Tony boomed. "'The Heromice in full force,' you say? My superdinosaurs will tear you to pieces!"

"We'll see about that, Sludge-face! You and your rebellious reptiles are no match for us!" Swiftpaws shouted.

"Heromice in action!"

TRAPPED!

Lady Wonderwhiskers, Swiftpaws, and I charged the Sewer Rats while One, Two, and Three lunged forward to try to grab us. We were on the verge of a superbattle when a piercing cry stopped us all.

"Stoooooop!"

Everybody froze, Heromice and Sewer Rats alike.

Teresa Sludge grabbed Tony's sleeve anxiously. "Oh, Sludgy," she howled.

"Wh-where's Elena?"

"Elena?" The head of the Sewer Rats' voice dropped. "Wasn't she with you?"

"No, I thought she was with *you*!" Teresa moaned.

"She can't still be —" Tony said with a TREMBLING voice.

"Our precious Elena! She's still in the mouseum!" Teresa began to SOB as Swiftpaws and I stood there stupefied.

Tony Sludge, EVIL head of the Sewer Rats, leader of all the sneaky rats in Rottington, and the teRRoR of all the citizens in Muskrat City, huddled next to his wife. He looked close to tears.

"My s-s-sweet Teresa," he mumbled. "You know I would never put you two in danger —"

Teresa shot a fierce look at her husband. "You fool! You good-for-nothing rat!

Our treasure is inside the mouseum with those **BEASTS**! If one of them touches one whisker on her, you'd better watch your tail!"

You good-for-nothing rat!

I-I'm sorry, my sweet.

"I promise w-we'll find her, Teresa," Tony stammered.

Catching the look of his henchmice, Tony cleared his throat and shot an **angry** glance at Slickfur. "Slickfur assured me that with the Animatronic Laser Ray, the superdinos would be under our control!"

Slickfur shrugged. "It's not my fault, boss. If you had listened to me when I explained how the laser ray worked . . ."

Beep!

Beep!

Beep!

The two Sewer Rats stopped arguing to **STARE** at me, or more accurately, my paw. For the love of pepper jack! What was happening?

It was my *communicator watch*! Proton had sent out an **EMERGENCY** call!

"Superstilton, come in! Superstilton, come in!" Proton shouted through my watch screen. "We need your help . . . *Bzz!* . . . we're trapped . . . *Bzz!* . . . in the . . . *Bzz!* . . . mouseum!"

Bzz! Bzz! Bzz!

Oh no! Proton's voice was breaking up from **interference**.

"Proton! Superstilton, here!" I responded excitedly. "Did you say 'we'? Who's with you?"

I **zoomed** in on the screen and couldn't believe my **EYES**.

"**Elena Sludge!**" Swiftpaws squealed as he peered over my shoulder.

Tony rushed over. "**Rotten ricotta!** Are you okay, my little cheese biscuit?"

"**UGH!**" Elena groaned. "If this **superugly** tyrannosaurus wasn't trying to eat me, everything would be just **swell**, Daddy."

"I'm sorry, my little **fur-face**. Daddy will be there to rescue you —"

Elena scowled. She was **MADDER** than a *wet* cat on a *cold* day. "Get me out of here!"

"Hey, move!" Proton protested. "I was

trying to talk to Superstilton!"

"Don't fight," I said. **SOUR CHEDDAR CHUNKS!** Rescuing these two was going to be tricky business. "The important thing is that you both get out of there."

"The *superpest* is right — for once!" Tony grumbled.

"Getting out is the problem," Proton explained. "A tyrannosaurus was chasing us, so we scurried down to the basement."

"Too bad there are no **exits** down here," Elena continued drily.

"Please . . . bzz . . . come save . . . bzz . . . us!" cried Proton. "And hurry!"

My screen went **black**. Tony and I looked at each other squeaklessly.

"Great f-fossilized f-fontina!" stuttered Swiftpaws. "We need a plan!"

Teresa Sludge crossed her paws across her

chest and GLARED at her husband. She
was angrier than a cat with fleas!

"This is all your fault, Sludgy," Teresa
said. "You'd better come up with something
fast!"

AN UNLIKELY TRUCE

Well, this was **new**. For the first time in Heromice history, we had the same **MISSION** as the Sewer Rats. We had to save the mouselings from the superdinos!

"Whether you like it or not, we must work **TOGETHER**!" said Lady Wonderwhiskers reasonably.

She was right. She always is, of course.

"I agree," I squeaked.

But Swiftpaws didn't want any part of it. "What in the name of **STRING CHEESE** do you mean, you want to work **with** the Sewer Rats?! We'll **NEVER** need the help of those sneaky thugs!"

"And the Sewer Rats will never need the

help of you **superfools**!" Tony grunted. "Never ever!"

"Please be reasonable, rodents," Lady Wonderwhiskers said calmly. "It's a **temporary** truce. Proton and Elena need us!"

"Yes, they're in incredible danger!" I echoed.

I won't hear of it!

Never ever!

Be reasonable, rodents . . .

"The superdinos are still **out of control** in the mouseum," she reminded them. "It won't be easy to get back in."

"We need to **unite**!" I concluded. "Time is running out! We need to find those rodents before the **TYRANNOSAURUS** beats us to it."

"What do you say, Mr. Sludge?" Lady Wonderwhiskers prodded. "How about you, Swiftpaws?"

Neither squeaked a word.

"Enough!" yelled Teresa. "The rodent in **blue** and the **red-caped** superfool are right!"

"Wh-what?!" Tony stammered.

"Remember, Sludgy," Teresa hissed. "If Elena gets hurt, I will hold you responsible! No more excuses! Bring back our daughter — *safe and sound*!"

"Argh!" he snarled. He shot a look at Commissioner Ratford, who was watching from a distance. "If you think working together means we'll let you A R R E S T us afterward, you are *HUGELY* mistaken!" He looked back at Swiftpaws. "Once we rescue Elena, we go back to being superenemies, agreed?!"

"Agreed . . ." my superpartner said as he shook Tony's paw. ". . . Sludgy!"

"Are you making fun of me?" Tony growled. "I'll crumble you like a block of

Gorgonzola! I'll **POUND** you like cheesy-bread dough!"

Tess interrupted them. "What if we used the Animatronic Laser Ray again and transformed the superdinosaurs back to statues?"

"Don't even think about it." Teresa sighed. "Tony left the **CONTRAPTION** inside the mouseum!"

"And even if we still had it," Slickfur added, "the effect of the laser ray can't be reversed. But it does **EXPIRE** after three hours."

Tess checked her watch. "An hour has already passed. That means the dinosaurs will return to being statues in **tWo HOURS**!"

"They could still do a lot of damage in two hours," I pointed out. "They could hurt

Proton and Elena. We have to stop them right away!"

"Of course!" Lady Wonderwhiskers agreed. "But we can't *totally* destroy them. They're **IMPORTANT** museum exhibits. We need to neutralize them somehow."

"Yes, but how?!" I exclaimed. I couldn't even tame a house cat. How would I **TAME** a tyrannosaurus?

Professor Ratosaurus approached us.

"If you need a **superexpert** on dinosaurs, I'm your mouse!" he said helpfully.

I'm your mouse!

THE GORGONZOLA TRAP

While our **MISSION** was to go back into the museum to save Proton and Elena, we had to face the dinosaurs surrounding us first.

"Take this, Superstilton." Tess fastened a strange bracelet to my wrist. "It could be useful."

"Huh? W-what is it?"

"It's a **Portable Hologram Projector**! If you point it at something, the device makes a copy and projects a *three-dimensional* image," Tess explained.

"Um . . . okay . . . but how do I use it?"

"Don't worry about that now," she responded. "We'll be monitoring you through your **communicator watch**. We'll help you when you need it!"

"And I'll be at your service," added the professor.

"Hurry, Superstilton!" said Swiftpaws. He was ready for *action*.

I watched as my superpartner headed up the mouseum stairs next to our greatest nemesis, Tony Sludge. That's a sight I thought I'd never see!

I turned to join them but found myself in front of two velociraptors rummaging in a trash can. As QUIET as a mouse in a barn full of cats, I called Professor Ratosaurus on my communicator watch.

"Avoid their **claws**," he advised.

"Velociraptors **slash** their prey."

Avoid their claws? He didn't have to tell me twice!

"There's also a theory that velociraptors **HUNTED** in packs," the professor added.

"I have an idea," Tess suggested. "Use the hologram projector to create a velociraptor pack leader."

"Great idea!" Professor Ratosaurus agreed.

Zap!

I pressed all the **buttons** on my special bracelet. "It's not working!" I squeaked.

Hearing my voice, the velociraptors shot their

heads up. They lunged toward me hungrily. I **banged** the buttons on my bracelet even faster.

ZAAAAP!

The projector finally activated. It produced a three-dimensional image of a giant velociraptor right in front of me.

The two real dinosaurs froze and stared

curiously at the new arrival.

"Th-they stopped . . ." I whispered.

"That's a good sign!" the professor replied. "Let's see if they think the **HOLOGRAM** is a pack leader. Try to get them to **follow** you somewhere we can trap them."

Roooaaarrr!

"B-but where?" I stuttered. "I need a **HUGE** space . . . one as big as the town square!"

"Hmm . . ." the professor muttered. He sounded as stumped as me. Then it came to me.

This way!

"But of course! SWISS SQUARE is under construction," I said, my ears twitching with excitement. "They just dug up a giant **hole**. I could trap the dinos there!"

I started making my way toward Swiss Square. To my amazement, the dinosaurs followed me. **Great balls of mozzarella!**

When the dinosaurs were nearing the **hole**, I made my holographic dino swerve. The velociraptors followed the image and **feLL** right into the construction hole.

But **blast**! The hole wasn't deep enough to contain them!

"Oh, **pickles and pizzas**!" Tess exclaimed. "You have to trap them, Superstilton!"

RATS! But how?

I racked my brain but couldn't come up with a thing. "**Great gobs of Gorgonzola**, I don't know how!" I shouted.

But with those words, my cheesy superpowers activated.

Plop! Plop! Plop! Plop!

Gooey gobs of Gorgonzola filled the hole, trapping the dinosaurs in a delicious mess.

MISSION ACCOMPLISHED!

I was heading back to the mouseum when

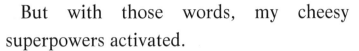

SUPERPOWER:
POOL OF GORGONZOLA
ACTIVATED WITH THE CRY:
"GREAT GOBS OF
GORGONZOLA!"

I saw a TRICERATOPS chasing Tony Sludge. The Sewer Rats' leader didn't look worried. He even slowed down to drop a small packet on the ground.

The Triceratops stepped on it a moment later.

WHAP! BAM!

The packet sprung open, transforming into a cage of indestructible steel. The triceratops was trapped!

"See that, superfool?" Tony growled. "The Sewer Rats always have a few tricks up our sleeves. Too bad we can't use them against you . . . for now!"

A FLYING SNACK

An incoming **communication** on my watch interrupted us.

"Great job with that velociraptor!" Swiftpaws congratulated me.

"Oh, well. Thanks. Um . . . where are you?"

"**Snouts up**, superpartner!"

Huh? I looked up. Chewy cheddar! Swiftpaws had transformed into a **YELLOW** kite and was flying over Swiss Square!

And he wasn't alone. A flock of pterodactyls was at his tail.

Snouts up!

"They've confused me with a flying snack!" my superpartner bellowed.

"I have a **PLAN**, Heromice!" Professor Ratosaurus's voice squeaked through my communicator watch. "The mouseum's solarium is detached from the rest of the building. Take

the **pterodactyls** there and LOCK them in!"

Swiftpaws *swooped* back over me. "Superstilton, did you get that? FLY to the roof of the solarium and wait for my Signal!"

"F-fly, you said? B-but I can't fly! I'm a 'fraidy

Follow me, you supersized birds!

mouse and I'm scared of heights!"

Swiftpaws ignored me. "This way, you SUPERSIZED birds!" he commanded the hungry dinosaurs.

MIGHTY PEPPERONI AND CHEESE BALLS! They were almost at the solarium! I had to get in position, so I gulped down my fear like a **cheddar cheese smoothie** and flew off.

Flap! Flap!

As soon as I landed on the **solarium** roof, I opened a large window. "Go, dinos! Go!"

Swiftpaws shot toward the open window with the **dinosaurs** in pursuit.

A few moments later, I heard a **crash**.

In you go!

"Be ready, **SUPERPARTNER**!" Swiftpaws shouted from inside.

One second, two seconds, two and a half seconds, three!

Swiftpaws came flying out and I **slammed** the roof window shut, locking the **dumbfounded** pterodactyls inside.

"**Mission accomplished**, superpartner!" Swiftpaws shouted, giving me a **Paw five**.

It was only then that I noticed how **high** up we were.

"I'm not a superpartner! I'm a **scaredy-mouse** and I want to get **down** from here!" I cried, my tail shaking.

"If you insist, I'll give you a **ride**, Superstilton," Swiftpaws offered.

We took off into the air and immediately

Here, boy!

saw Lady Wonderwhiskers
dealing with a stegosaurus!

"Here, boy!" said the
FEARLESS super-
rodent. Then she launched
an *elastic rope* from
her supercostume sleeve.
With a **FLICK** of her

paw, the rope wrapped around the legs of the stegosaurus and tied them up tightly.

The superdino tried to move, but it tripped and landed with a loud **THUD**.

"SUPER STRING CHEESE!" exclaimed Swiftpaws. "Nice hit!"

"Tess Technopaws deserves the credit," she squeaked. "She invented the rubber leash!"

Ah, Lady Wonderwhiskers . . . She was so BRAVE and so humble . . .

But there was no time to dwell. In the next moment, Commissioner Ratford and Professor Ratosaurus passed by. They were waving carrots, celery, lettuce, and radishes under the nose of a mammoth brontosaurus.

The beast was following

nom, nom, nom!

them docilely.
ASTOUNDING!
How had that
happened?

"He's a
vegetarian,"
the professor said with a
smile. "He may be massive, but
he's really quite **harmless**."

"We're taking him to the park where
he can **SNACK** on some trees and stay out
of trouble," Ratford added. "Then we can
finally rescue Proton and Elena!"

TYRANNOSAURUS HIDE-AND-SEEK

Over at the mouseum, Proton and Elena were still hiding out in the basement among the **dusty** boxes of exhibits in storage.

"At least we have these boxes of junk to hide us," Elena commented.

"Junk?!" Proton exclaimed. "These are **valuable historical artifacts**!"

"Don't tell me you're one of those smarty-mice who spend all their time reading **books**," she said with disdain.

"Well, no . . ." he replied. "But what's wrong with **BOOKS**?"

ROOOaaaRRR!

A hungry tyrannosaurus entering the basement interrupted the two mice.

"Oh no!" shrieked Proton.

"Shhh!" hissed Elena.

The dinosaur **SNIFFED** the air and headed in their direction.

The dinosaur swiped at the boxes hiding the mouselets with its sharp claws.

Sniff, sniff, sniff...

The boxes fell to the floor with a loud

CRAAASH!

Just in time, Proton and Elena scurried behind another pile of boxes. When the dino's back was turned, Elena *crawled* toward the stairs across the room.

"Hey!" Proton whispered. "What are you doing?"

"My dear nerd, I don't know what you're doing, but as long as that thing is **down** here, I want to be **UP** there!" she said gesturing to the stairs.

"But that's too far away," Proton warned. "It'll see you!"

"You know what, SUPERNERD?" Elena replied. "It beats hiding here!"

Suddenly, the shadow of the super-tyrannosaurus loomed over the boxes hiding Proton. He gulped. Could this be the end of his short life?

crash! Thud! Bonk!

As she tried to escape, Elena knocked over a box of prehistoric bird bones. The dinosaur's attention shifted. Now the giant dino was focused on her instead of Proton! The ferocious beast turned toward her and charged.

"Aaaah! Help!" Elena shrieked. "Don't eat me! Sewer Rats taste DISGUSTING! Wouldn't you like to taste a deliciously intelligent rodent like my friend Proton instead?"

The T. rex simply roared in reply. Then it leaned down, Jaws opened wide . . .

SPLASH!

A **sprinkler** had sprung open and a stream of ICE-COLD water gushed right on the dino's head!

"Elena, let's get out of here!" shouted Proton.

"H-how did you do that?" Elena asked in AMAZEMENT. "How did you **save** me?"

Proton shrugged. "I just activated the **fire alarm**," he said, pointing to the electric panel behind him. "I read how to do it . . . in a **book**."

For a moment, Elena looked impressed. But after a second, her usual scowl returned.

Proton cleared his throat. "Anyway, uh . . . have no fear." He pointed to the ceiling. "We can **hide** in the ventilation duct."

Elena looked skeptical. "Are you sure

about that, **smarty-mouse**?"

"Do you have a better idea?" he shot back. "We'll be **safe** up there . . . I think."

Rooooaaarrr!!!

The tyrannosaurus had recovered from its *cold shower* and was back on track.

"Come on, Elena!" Proton called. "There's no time to lose!"

"Okay!" Elena agreed. "It doesn't look like we have any other options."

The two mice **RACED** up a pile of boxes. Proton opened the ventilation duct door and pulled up Elena. They **slammed** the vent closed just as the tyrannosaurus tried to **CHOMP** her tail. **WHEW!**

"That was a close call," Proton said with a sigh.

Elena just **scowled**.

"Well, smart stuff," she huffed. "Now that we're up here, what's our next move?"

Proton was silent. He had no *clue* what to do next!

Come on!

Hurry!

SWIFTPAWS'S PLAN

Swiftpaws, Lady Wonderwhiskers, and I were ready to go into the mouseum at last when a beastly unfamiliar-looking dinosaur blocked us.

"Peppery Parmesan!" Swiftpaws exclaimed. "What's *this* creature?!"

"It's an **allosaurus**!" the professor shouted through my communicator watch. "Be careful, friends. The allosaurus is a **nasty** predator."

Proving the professor's point, the allosaurus charged toward us.

"Superboots, power up!" Lady Wonderwhiskers shouted. "Fire gumballs!"

SUPERWOW! Hundreds of large **gumballs** shot out of the toes of Lady Wonderwhiskers' boots, covering the floor.

The allosaurus took another step. But the slippery gumballs made him TRIP, slide, twirl, TUMBLE, and crash to the ground!

"Nice move, Lady Wonderwhiskers!" I cheered. Ah, Lady Wonderwhiskers. Always so *quick* on her paws . . .

"The coast is clear, superpartners!" Swiftpaws announced.

But maybe he had squeaked too soon.

The superdino had found its legs and was after us again.

"Oh no!" I cried. "He's back! FOR A THOUSAND POUNDS OF PECORINO!"

At those words, a huge **monster-sized** wheel of Pecorino materialized above the allosaurus and fell down on its head, knocking it out.

"Wonderful!" squeaked the lady rodent of my dreams.

"Oh, well, uh . . . thanks!" I **blushed**.

But how could it be? The determined dino was up and after us *again*!

"Wait! Wh-where's **Swiftpaws**?!" I cried, my tail tying in *knots*.

"I'm right here, superpartner!" replied a voice from behind me.

I turned and saw Swiftpaws aboard a **tanker truck**.

"Wh-what are

**SUPERPOWER:
MONSTER-SIZED WHEEL
OF PECORINO
ACTIVATED WITH THE CRY:
"FOR A THOUSAND
POUNDS OF PECORINO!"**

we going to do with that?!" I yelped.

"You'll see!" He parked the truck and hopped out. Then he ran to the side and unrolled a hose connected to the tank. Next, Swiftpaws pointed the hose at the allosaurus.

Sploosh! Slop! Slop!

The hose squirted a stream of supersticky cheese sauce in the allosaurus's face! Superdino-melt on toast! The creature was trapped in a gooey mess.

Care for a snack?

In no time, the dinosaur was on its back, completely **tangled** in clumps of cheese.

Swiftpaws grinned. "Now that's a DELICIOUS victory!"

It was a *tasty* victory — for the moment. But we **still** had to get back to the mouseum!

Ugh!

THAT'S A MOUTHFUL

Our path was clear, and we **finally** made it inside the mouseum, where we met up with Tony, Slickfur, and their henchmice.

"What are we waiting for?" Tony grunted. "Elena is **trapped** in the basement. Let's go!"

"The *Heromice* will lead the way!" announced Swiftpaws.

Heh, heh, heh...

"No, the Sewer Rats will go first!" said One in a booming voice. Then he stormed off.

We followed the Sewer Rats as they trudged through the mouseum halls and down to the vast basement.

"**Elena!**" Tony shouted. "Where are you?"

"**Proton!**" I yelled. "Are you in here?"

Elena!

My **EYES** were on the lookout for any superdinos while my h:eart thumped inside my fur. Then I heard a familiar voice.

"Superstilton! Swiftpaws! Lady Wonderwhiskers!"

Proton!

"It's Proton!" Swiftpaws exclaimed.

"And his voice is coming from . . . the ventilation duct!" Lady Wonderwhiskers added. She pointed above us.

Cheese and crackers! Above our heads, we could see Proton's snout peeking through the vent.

"We hid up here to escape from the *tyrannosaurus*," Proton explained.

"But now we're **STUCK** and can't move. **Ugh!**" Elena said with disgust.

Swiftpaws puffed up his chest. "Don't worry, mouselets! We'll get you out of there **PRONTO**!"

"Uh . . . I'm afraid you'll have to deal with *it* first." Proton said, turning **whiter** than a slice of mozzarella.

"I-it?" I asked, my whiskers twitching.

ROOOaaaRRR! ROO

Trembling in fear, I turned to see the **ferocious** tyrannosaurus looming over us.

It was much **BIGGER** than the allosaurus. And it was much **angrieR**, too!

Lady Wonderwhiskers tried using the **rubber leash**, but the tyrannosaurus broke it with just one step.

Oops . . .

Whoosh!

"Leave this to me, SUPERPESTS!" Tony Sludge shouted. He pulled out a strange **contraption**. "I'll trap it with my insta-net!"

A net flew out of the device and landed on the dinosaur's large head. But the dino bit through the net with its SUPERSHARP teeth in an instant.

Swiftpaws and I looked at each other. "This reptile isn't **BiG** enough to **scare** us, right, superpartner?" he asked.

Uh-oh.

I was too **terrified** to answer! But Swiftpaws didn't lose heart. Instead, he shouted our battle cry: **"Heromice in action!"**

Then he called to me, "Superstilton, you distract the beast!"

"D-distract it?! B-but h-how can I distract a massive **prehistoric** monster?!"

"You're a **smart** mouse," he said encouragingly. "Come up with something!"

Then he yelled, "Costume: *Muzzle Mode!*"

In a second, my friend had transformed into a supersized *yellow* muzzle. Now all he needed was the right time to clamp down on the superdino's jaws.

"Superstilton, you're up!" called Lady Wonderwhiskers. "Try to keep it still!"

"B-but I don't know how!" I yelled back. **"Great balls of mozzarella!"**

With those words, my **superpowers** activated. A flurry of chewy mozzarella balls **bombarded** the tyrannosaurus and filled its wide-open mouth.

RAHRGGG! MMFFF . . .

After a few seconds, the beast's mouth was so full of cheese that it couldn't chomp down on anything!

"With its razor-sharp teeth, it won't take long for him to **chew** through that mozzarella," **Professor Ratosaurus** pointed out.

"We need to think of something else fast!"
cried Swiftpaws.

"We won't need to," Slickfur said, looking

Take that!

SUPERPOWER:
MOZZARELLA GAG
ACTIVATED WITH
THE CRY:
"GREAT BALLS OF
MOZZARELLA!"

95

at the **CLOCK**. "We just need a few more **seconds**: seven, six, five, four . . ."

The tyrannosaurus had chewed and spit out the last of the mozzarella. He was looming over our heads when —

". . . three, two, one!"

The dinosaur **froze**.

"Exactly three hours have passed!" Slickfur explained with a satisfied grin. "The effects of the Animatronic Laser Ray have expired!"

Swiftpaws couldn't control his **CURIOSITY**. He cautiously approached the beast and touched its claw.

"He's right! It's as **harmless** as a block of cheddar," he announced. "Mission accomplished!"

It's harmless!

ENEMIES AGAIN

Not so fast. We still had to get Proton and Elena out of the ventilation duct!

"Ah, no problem," Swiftpaws said. "Costume: Ladder Mode!"

As he transformed into a tall yellow ladder, Lady Wonderwhiskers nudged me with her paw.

"Go ahead, Superstilton," she said.

"B-but why m-me? That's a very TALL ladder and I'm a-afraid of heights!"

Sigh. I couldn't disappoint the wondrous super-rodent, so I took a DEEP breath.

Then I climbed the ladder, unfastened the grate (Oof! It sure was heavy!), grabbed Proton, and started to yank him out.

"Wait, hold on, Superstilton," the young

mouse squeaked.

"I've got you!" I declared, ignoring the **wiggly** ladder. "We're almost out —"

"Stop! Superstilton, helllp!"

Help!

Aaah!

WHaaa! CRASH!

"**Ow!**" I mumbled, crawling out from under Proton.

Proton stood up and rubbed his tail while Lady Wonderwhiskers climbed up the ladder and helped Elena out.

"Great cheddar!" Swiftpaws exclaimed. "We did it! Now we can relax!"

"Relax?!" Tony guffawed. "Don't make me laugh!"

Slickfur had recovered the Animatronic Laser Ray and returned it to Tony.

Put down the laser!

"Wait, what are you doing? We have a truce, remember?!" I squeaked.

"I remember." He **SMIRKED**. "We agreed to work together until Proton and Elena were rescued. Then we said we would return to being *superenemies*!"

I looked at my friends. We couldn't let the Sewer Rats use the ray ever again. The **city** could be destroyed!

Paws up, Heromice!

"Put down the laser ray, sewer trash, or you'll be sorry!" Swiftpaws demanded.

Slickfur responded by launching a *ball of string* that opened into a huge net.

WHOOSH!

A second later, Swiftpaws, Lady Wonderwhiskers, and I were wrapped up so tight we couldn't move a **whisker**.

"Do something, Swiftpaws!" I yelped.

"Costume: SCISSOR MODE!"

Snip, snip, snip!

Swiftpaws cut us out **QUICKLY**, but

our troubles weren't over.

Tony Sludge was getting away with the laser ray, and One, Two, and Three were blocking our path.

"Stop! Give us that laser ray **now**!" Lady Wonderwhiskers shouted as she skillfully **dodged** the henchmice.

"Never!" roared the Sewer Rats' boss. "Take it, Slickfur!"

He tossed the superdino-making ray to his right-hand mouse. But it passed through Slickfur as if he were a **GHOST** — and landed right in my paws.

"For a thousand **MUSKY** cats, how did that happen?!" Tony yelled to his assistant.

"Boss, I'm over here!" said a voice.

Tony turned around and saw **another** Slickfur **behind** him! "Huh? What's going on?!"

"You can blame yourself, Sludge," I explained. "You thought you were throwing the device to Slickfur — but it was a copy of him that I made with Tess's Portable Hologram Projector!"

Lady Wonderwhiskers shot an admiring look at me. I almost melted like a slice of Swiss on a hot panini press.

It only lasted a moment, but it made my HEART skip a beat. Then I remembered our problem and I turned my attention back to Tony Sludge.

"Don't move another paw, Sludge!" I cried. "You have no way out!"

BROKEN PROMISES

To all of our **SURPRISE**, I was wrong!

Vroom!

Suddenly, the **Sludgemobile** tunneled up through the ground.

"Elena! Tony! Here I am, darlings!" Teresa Sludge cried from behind the steering wheel.

She **SQUEALED** excitedly when she saw her family. "Elena, my treasure! Sludgy! Are you okay? Get in!"

Elena! Tony! Here I am, darlings!

The Sewer Rats rushed over to the car. Before hopping in, Tony grinned. "Till next time, **Losermice**! Just remember: Slickfur can always make another **Animatronic Laser Ray**! Har, har, har!"

Teresa glared at her husband. "Not if you want to keep your **FUR**, Sludgy!"

"B-but, Teresa . . ." Tony stammered.

"No *buts*! Elena only escaped by a whisker. This is the **END** for that device or I'm going home without you!"

Tony sighed. "Yes, dear . . ."

Teresa smiled smugly. She looked like a **cat** at a canary party.

Elena was getting in the car when she stopped and strode over to Proton.

"Well, *smarty-mouse*. I'll see you later." She **smiled** ever so slightly. "It wasn't the worst getting **STUCK** with you."

Proton shrugged. "Ahem, well, uh . . ."

But the young rat was already in the car. From the open window, she smiled at Proton. Then she put her paw to her snout and blew him a **KiSS**.

Proton turned as **red** as a tomato as the **Sludgemobile** burrowed back underground.

When Commissioner Ratford and his agents entered the hall, the only sign of the Sewer Rats was the **HOLE** the Sludgemobile had left behind.

"Drat! They **escaped** again!" said the exasperated police chief.

I tried to think of a SILVER LINING. "Well, at least everything can get back to normal . . ."

To squeak the truth, things weren't exactly like before. The mouseum looked

Puff! Pant!

like a **HURRICANE** had passed through it! Slowly, Professor Ratosaurus and the mouseum staff returned the dinosaur models to their places.

Swiftpaws transformed into a bulldozer and we went to retrieve the velociraptor models from the hole in **Swiss Square**.

"**Jurassic cream cheese and jelly!**" Swiftpaws exclaimed as he scooped up the dino. "There's so much to do!"

Meanwhile, Proton was feeling topsy-turvy from Elena's affections.

"Pickles and Parmesan! Are you okay?" Tess inquired. "You're **flushed**!"

"Everything is, uh . . . j-just fine," Proton stuttered. "It was an in-incredible adventure."

"Yes, yes, and now that it's over, I have only one **REGRET**!" Swiftpaws said.

Everyone looked at him curiously.

"In all this **pandemonium**, Superstilton didn't get to give his SPEECH!"

"Oh, uh, that's just fine," I said. "In fact, it's more than fine!"

Proton, Electron, Tess, and Lady Wonderwhiskers burst out laughing.

And with that, it was time for me to return to

Are you okay?

Hugs!

New Mouse City.
I said good-bye to my friends and activated my supercostume.

Whoosh!

I flew back to New Mouse City and landed in the garden of the *Mouseum of Modern Art.*

The opening **GALA** of Andy Mousehol's exhibit was long over. But I still had to *write* my feature article for *The Rodent's Gazette*!

See you soon, my friends!

As I looked at the artist's wacky sculptures, I wondered what would have happened if the Sewer Rats had used the laser ray on these artworks. New Mouse City would have been invaded by animated phone booths!

Yikes! The idea made me WOOZY. I had had enough of objects brought to **life**.

Come to think of it: After my *DINO-SIZED ADVENTURE*, writing an article on Andy Mousehol's baffling art seemed as **EASY** as cheese pie.

Whether it's a deadline or a deadly dino, **nothing can stop the Heromice!** Till next time!

Be sure to read all my fabumouse adventures!

#1 Lost Treasure of the Emerald Eye

#2 The Curse of the Cheese Pyramid

#3 Cat and Mouse in a Haunted House

#4 I'm Too Fond of My Fur!

#5 Four Mice Deep in the Jungle

#6 Paws Off, Cheddarface!

#7 Red Pizzas for a Blue Count

#8 Attack of the Bandit Cats

#9 A Fabumouse Vacation for Geronimo

#10 All Because of a Cup of Coffee

#11 It's Halloween, You 'Fraidy Mouse!

#12 Merry Christmas, Geronimo!

#13 The Phantom of the Subway

#14 The Temple of the Ruby of Fire

#15 The Mona Mousa Code

#16 A Cheese-Colored Camper

#17 Watch Your Whiskers, Stilton!

#18 Shipwreck on the Pirate Islands

#19 My Name Is Stilton, Geronimo Stilton

#20 Surf's Up, Geronimo!

#21 The Wild, Wild West

#22 The Secret of Cacklefur Castle

A Christmas Tale

#23 Valentine's Day Disaster

#24 Field Trip to Niagara Falls

#25 The Search for Sunken Treasure

#26 The Mummy with No Name

#27 The Christmas Toy Factory

#28 Wedding Crasher

#29 Down and Out Down Under

#30 The Mouse Island Marathon

#31 The Mysterious Cheese Thief

Christmas Catastrophe

#32 Valley of the Giant Skeletons

#33 Geronimo and the Gold Medal Mystery

#34 Geronimo Stilton, Secret Agent

#35 A Very Merry Christmas

#36 Geronimo's Valentine

#37 The Race Across America

#38 A Fabumouse School Adventure

#39 Singing Sensation

#40 The Karate Mouse

#41 Mighty Mount Kilimanjaro

#42 The Peculiar Pumpkin Thief

#43 I'm Not a Supermouse!

#44 The Giant Diamond Robbery

#45 Save the White Whale!

#46 The Haunted Castle

#47 Run for the Hills, Geronimo!

#48 The Mystery in Venice

#49 The Way of the Samurai

#50 This Hotel Is Haunted!

#51 The Enormouse Pearl Heist

#52 Mouse in Space!

#53 Rumble in the Jungle

#54 Get into Gear, Stilton!

#55 The Golden Statue Plot

#56 Flight of the Red Bandit

Special Edition!

The Hunt for the Golden Book

#57 The Stinky Cheese Vacation

#58 The Super Chef Contest

#59 Welcome to Moldy Manor

Special Edition!

The Hunt for the Curious Cheese

#60 The Treasure of Easter Island

#61 Mouse House Hunter

#62 Mouse Overboard!

Special Edition!

The Hunt for the Secret Papyrus

#63 The Cheese Experiment

#64 Magical Mission

#65 Bollywood Burglary

Special Edition!

The Hunt for the Hundredth Key

MEET
Geronimo Stiltonord

He is a mouseking — the Geronimo Stilton of the ancient far north! He lives with his brawny and brave clan in the village of Mouseborg. From sailing frozen waters to facing fiery dragons, every day is an adventure for the micekings!

#1 Attack of the Dragons

#2 The Famouse Fjord Race

#3 Pull the Dragon's Tooth!

Be sure to read all of our magical special edition adventures!

THE KINGDOM OF FANTASY

THE QUEST FOR PARADISE:
THE RETURN TO THE KINGDOM OF FANTASY

THE AMAZING VOYAGE:
THE THIRD ADVENTURE IN THE KINGDOM OF FANTASY

THE DRAGON PROPHECY:
THE FOURTH ADVENTURE IN THE KINGDOM OF FANTASY

THE VOLCANO OF FIRE:
THE FIFTH ADVENTURE IN THE KINGDOM OF FANTASY

THE SEARCH FOR TREASURE:
THE SIXTH ADVENTURE IN THE KINGDOM OF FANTASY

THE ENCHANTED CHARMS:
THE SEVENTH ADVENTURE IN THE KINGDOM OF FANTASY

THE PHOENIX OF DESTINY:
AN EPIC KINGDOM OF FANTASY ADVENTURE

THE HOUR OF MAGIC:
THE EIGHTH ADVENTURE IN THE KINGDOM OF FANTASY

THE WIZARD'S WAND:
THE NINTH ADVENTURE IN THE KINGDOM OF FANTASY

THE JOURNEY THROUGH TIME

BACK IN TIME:
THE SECOND JOURNEY THROUGH TIME

THE RACE AGAINST TIME:
THE THIRD JOURNEY THROUGH TIME

LOST IN TIME:
THE FOURTH JOURNEY THROUGH TIME

Meet
GERONIMO STILTONOOT

He is a cavemouse—Geronimo Stilton's ancient ancestor! He runs the stone newspaper in the prehistoric village of Old Mouse City. From dealing with dinosaurs to dodging meteorites, his life in the Stone Age is full of adventure!

#1 The Stone of Fire

#2 Watch Your Tail!

#3 Help, I'm in Hot Lava!

#4 The Fast and the Frozen

#5 The Great Mouse Race

#6 Don't Wake the Dinosaur!

#7 I'm a Scaredy-Mouse!

#8 Surfing for Secrets

#9 Get the Scoop, Geronimo!

#10 My Autosaurus Will Win!

#11 Sea Monster Surprise

#12 Paws Off the Pearl!

#13 The Smelly Search

DEAR MOUSE FRIENDS,
THANKS FOR READING, AND
FAREWELL TILL THE NEXT BOOK.
IT'LL BE ANOTHER
WHISKER-LICKING-GOOD
ADVENTURE, AND THAT'S
A PROMISE!